The Moose Family

Roaming the Forests, Footloose and Free

LONNIE SCHORER

Illustrated by Christopher Gorey

THIS BOOK BELONGS TO

_____

Are you in the mood to meet a moose,
A 4-footed, foraging guy on the loose?
A footloose moose is faster than a goose.

Mighty Max is his name,
King of the Forest is his fame.
This famous footloose moose named Max,
Follows narrow, winding, wooded tracks.

In northern woods both deep and dark,
Max munches beech twigs, birch and bark.
This stick munching, bark crunching mighty moose
Blends into shadows beneath stately spruce.

Roaming the wilds without compass or map,
Max settled down for an afternoon nap.
Dreaming moose dreams short and sweet,
Of succulent meadow stalks ripe to eat.

In this meadow so broad and hilly,
Stood a vision, a beautiful filly,
A 4-footed footloose, fancy-free Millie,
Pretty as the blush on a springtime lily.

Millie Moose, so kind and so fair,
Was a friend to all, from swallow to bear.
Sharing her knowledge of dens and berries,
She told them stories of owls and fairies.

When Max asked Millie if she would wed.
For love had gone straight to his head,
Millie wore a lavender garland of myrtle,
Woven for her by Thatcher the Turtle.

To the wedding of Max and Millie Moose,
George the Snake escorted Golly Goose.
Squirrels brought pine nuts and Otter — some juice,
While Sly Fox came with the Churkendoose.

Humming moose melodies all in tune,
They danced the foxtrot by the light of the moon.
A toast was given by Ralph Raccoon
On this merriest night in the month of June.

But meandering moose rarely stay in one place,
Traveling many a mile at an astonishing pace.
So Max and Millie bid farewell to their friends,
And headed off with their odds and their ends.

Animals gathered to honor the pair,
While waving white blossoms high in the air —
A traditional send-off for those who dare,
Leave the verdant cover of a shrubberied lair.

The moose migrated north, south, east and west,
With might and muscles put to test.
Through snowy storms and howling gales,
They held their course and blazed new trails.

Fording rivers and lakes, marshes and ponds,
They waded between grasses and cattail fronds.
Staying together with brains granite strong,
They knew what was right and what was wrong.

Raise the flag and sound the horn!
To Max and Millie a son is born.
Tall and true, a miniature Max,
They nudged his nose and named him Jax.

Jax learned his A's, B's, and trees,
And to say yes thanks and please.
Faster than any fleet-footed fawn,
He never rested from dusk until dawn.

Quick jumping Jax's footloose feet
Had places to go and friends to meet.
Beneath the cliff edge tall and steep,
He lost his way in the forest deep.

Lightning sparked and thunder rolled,
Wet, wet rains made nighttime cold.
He missed his comfy, leafy bed,
He missed a pine pillow for his head.

What should he do, where should he go?
How is a young loose moose to know?
Manny Mose-of-the-Mountain high above,
Whispered a message of comfort and love.

Animals quickly spread the news,
While hawks speculated and crows gave their views.
Chittering to debate and chattering to amuse,
They relayed the facts and followed the clues.

His parents' words rang in his ear,
Don't wander far, please stay near!
What's that? A voice! Can you hear?
A long forest echo, loud and clear.

J-A-X-um-um-um, J-A-X-um-um-um,
It's DA-dum-dum-dum, DA-dum-dum-dum.
Where are YOU-you-you-you?
The animals have come to your RES-cue-ue-ue.

Max led the team when Jax was found,
Returning him to Millie, safe and sound.
Footloose moose can romp and roam,
But best by far is the place called home.

Days were full for the moose family,
With so much to do and so much to see.
Max and Jax and sweet Millie,
Exploring the world, footloose and free.

Mountains majestic and plains so wide,
Rainbows and sunsets, the swell of the tide,
New things they found and dared and tried,
As they studied and learned with wisdom and pride.

Among the miracles of life on Earth,
Are Love and Laughter, Joy and Birth.
Each moose born is unlike another,
One starry night Jax had a brother!

The smallest moose's name was Sam,
Long as a log and strong as a ram.
With quiet wonder in his eyes,
He felt the warmth of family ties.

Wrapped in love from his head to his feet,
Mini-moose Sam liked to sleep and to eat.
One day he'd be as tall and mighty as Max,
But now he just wants to imitate Jax.

Early birds sang the good morning song,
Trilling wakey-wakey, don't sleep so long.
Bluebell blossoms rang ding-dong, ding-dong,
The forest chorus was surprisingly strong.

Each day the brothers raced and rumbled,
Helping each other when one of them stumbled.
They rolled bocce stones with the sound bink-bonk,
Until tucked in at night with a quiet dink-donk.

Sam and Jax learned with a guiding hand,
The paths in the forest, the feel of the sand.
The rhythm of breezes, the ways of the land,
Where to find patience and how to understand.

Meeting each challenge in their quest,
They all worked hard and tried their best,
To Imagine and Risk, to Discover and Explore!
Their mantra can help us to grow and to soar.

With 16 fleet-footed-footstrong feet,
The magnificent moose family now is complete,
And someday, when you are in a moosely mode,
You may just see them crossing the road.

If we could wish and wave a wand,
To travel to endless horizons beyond,
We might know what their future will bring,
But wait, there's a time and a place for everything.

And now it's time to go to sleep, with memories of this day to keep.
"God bless you, keep you and watch over you, and may you have a
lovely sleep."

Writer's note:

This tale was jotted in a hot summer's heat,
After Nonnie and Gigi a moose did meet.
They'd just said they were_in the mood to meet a moose,
A 4-footed, foraging guy on the loose.
Or, was it but a dream?

Topics for discussion:

Millie helped the bear.
- Have you ever helped someone you didn't know very well?
- Have you ever been shy about asking for help?

The moose couple decided to move to find a new home.
- Have you ever moved?
- Was it difficult to say goodbye to your old friends, and was it hard to make new ones?

Jax has a younger brother.
- If you have younger brothers or sisters, do you help them learn how to do things?
- Are you patient when they try to follow you and do everything you do?

Jax wandered off and lost his way in the forest.
- Have you ever been lost?
- Were you frightened, and are you able to describe the experience?

Jax's parents advised him to stay close to home.
- Why is it important to listen to your parents?
- Was there a time you didn't listen to your parents and something happened?

Young Jax got caught in a storm.
- Why is it a good idea to check the weather before leaving on a camping trip or hike?
- Thunderstorms can be loud. Are you afraid of storms? Why?

The moose family experienced sunsets and mountains and flowers and birds.

- Do you take time to notice and appreciate nature's beauty?
- Are you able to color or paint a picture of a sunrise or a sunset?

Exploring doesn't have to be hiking into the woods. Exploring can be via books and learning!

- Where do you go to explore, and why do you think it's important to keep exploring?
- Are you able to name some famous explorers?

If you are faced with a challenge, how do you respond?

- Do you give up without trying, or do you try to stay calm and think of ways to handle it?
- Even when you are not sure of the outcome, do you try to do your best?

Written at Lake Winnipesaukee for Jackson and Sammy by their grandmother "Nonnie", after a twilight moose encounter on a North Sandwich, New Hampshire road on July 1, 2002. Jackson — 2 years and 10 months old — and Sammy — 13 days old - live faraway in Colorado where there are many, many moose to meet.

CPSIA information can be obtained
at www.ICGtesting.com
Printed in the USA
BVHW091653010719
552376BV00015B/189/P